Stone soup
and other stories

Stone soup   page 3

Poor old horse   page 13

Cinderella   page 23

M
Macmillan Education

The publishers would like to thank the following
for their stories:
Joan Wyatt for Stone soup, illustrated by Tony Kenyon.
Ron Deadman for Poor old horse, illustrated by Val Biro.
Ron Deadman for Cinderella, illustrated by Sara Silcock.
Editorial Consultant: Donna Bailey

First published 1987

Published by
MACMILLAN EDUCATION LTD
Houndmills, Basingstoke, Hampshire RG21 2XS
and London
Companies and representatives
throughout the world

Cover design by The Design Works, Reading

Printed and bound in Spain by
Gráficas Estella, S. A. Navarra.

British Library Cataloguing in Publication Data
Wyatt, Joan, 1934–
Stone soup; and, other stories.—(New Way)
1.Readers—1950-
I.Title   II.Deadman, Ronald
428.6   PE1119
ISBN 0–333–41886–7

Stone soup

One day a poor man walked over the hill.
He came to the rich man's house and
knocked on the door.

"Please will you give me some water?" he said.

"To drink?" said the rich man.

"No, to cook," said the poor man. "I need it
to make stone soup."

Now the rich man never gave something
for nothing.

"Can I have some soup?" he said
to the poor man.

"Of course," said the poor man. "You are
very welcome. Come and sit by my fire."

The rich man poured some water into a jug and
gave it to the poor man.
They went to the poor man's house and
the rich man sat down by the fire.
The poor man took his cooking pot and
put a small stone in the bottom.
He poured the water into the pot and
set it on the fire to cook.
For a while the water was still,
then it began to bubble.

"We must wait," said the poor man.
"Cooking takes time."

The rich man had never made soup.
He had eaten a lot of soup but
he did not know how to make it.
He began to feel hungry.

"Will it be long?" he said.

"It's quicker with a ham bone,"
said the poor man.

So the rich man ran to his house
to look for a ham bone.
He looked on every shelf and in every
cupboard. He looked in every pot and pan.
At last he came back.

"Will this do?" he said. "I can only find
a chicken."

"Well," said the poor man. "A chicken is not
the same as a ham bone, but it may do."

He put the chicken in the pot.
For a moment the water was still, and then
it began to bubble again.

"Is it almost ready?" said the rich man.

"Almost," said the poor man. "Of course,
it's quicker with an onion."

The rich man ran to his house again.
He came back with three onions.

"Will these do?" he said.

"Well," said the poor man. "Three onions
are not the same as one, but they may do."

He cut the onions up and put them in the pot.
For a moment the water was still, and then
it began to bubble again.

The rich man sniffed.
He could smell the chicken cooking.
He could smell the onions.
He did feel hungry. "Is it ready now?" he said.

"Almost," said the poor man. "Of course,
it's quicker with . . ."

"What?" said the rich man, who was really
hungry now. "What's it quicker with?"

"It's quicker with an old carrot or two,"
said the poor man.

The rich man ran to his house.
He knew where to look now.
He came back with a bag of carrots,
all fresh and orange.

"Will these do?" he said.

"They are a bit new," said the poor man.
"But they may do."

He put the carrots in the pot.
The soup was still, and then
it began to bubble again.

"It smells ready," said the rich man.

"Yes," said the poor man, stirring the soup with his wooden spoon.

The rich man licked his lips. "Now?" he said.

"No," said the poor man. "I forgot the potatoes."

In a moment the rich man ran to his house. In a moment he was back with a sack of potatoes.

"Only a few," said the poor man. "No need to be greedy."

In next to no time the soup began to bubble again.

"Now?" said the rich man.

"Now for the secret," said the poor man.

He took a small box from his pocket.

He shook out some salt.

"Never," he said, "never forget the salt."

The rich man nodded.

He would never forget the salt.

He had never felt so hungry in his life.

"Now?" he said.

"Yes," said the poor man. He dipped
his wooden spoon into the soup.

"Have a taste," he said. "Be careful, it's hot!"

By now the rich man was very hungry.
Both men ate the soup up fast.
Soon only the stone was left
at the bottom of the pot.
The two men looked at each other.
They felt happy and full.
"That was good soup," said the rich man.
"The best," said the poor man.
The rich man looked at the stone in
the bottom of the pot.
"You can have it," said the poor man.
"I can find another."

The rich man took the stone quickly.
He smiled. "Thank you," he said. "I must tell
my cook how to make stone soup."

"You're welcome," said the poor man.
"Don't forget the salt."

He licked his fingers and
tied his cooking pot to his pack,
then he walked away over the hill.

Poor old horse

Many years ago, a good, kind King lived
in his palace near a town called Atri.
When the people of the town were cold
or hungry, the King sent them food or
logs for their fires.
The King wanted everyone to be happy.
He looked after his people and
his people loved him.

One day the King said to himself,
"How will I know if someone in the town
needs my help?"

Then the King had an idea.
He told his men to hang a big bell
high up in a tower.
Then he told them to tie
a long rope to the bell.
The bell-rope reached all the way
to the ground.

Then the King said to his people,
"If you ever need my help, you must
pull the rope. That will ring the bell.
Then I will come and help you."

Many years went by and
the rope became very old.
It kept on breaking.
   "Make a new rope," said the King.
   While the new rope was being made,
his men hung a long grape vine in its place.
The vine was covered with
beautiful green leaves.

In the town of Atri lived a man
called Antonio.
He had an old horse called Stefano.
Stefano had worked for Antonio for many years,
but now he was too old to work any more.
Antonio was a cruel man, so when he saw
that Stefano was too old to work,
he sent him away.

Stefano walked through the streets of Atri
looking for something to eat.
Sometimes he ate grass or leaves, but
there was not much grass in the town.
The poor old horse was always cold and hungry.

As the days went by, he grew
thinner and thinner.
Then one day Stefano saw something
which looked good to eat.
He saw the green leaves on the grape vine.
    "I have found something to eat at last,"
he said to himself and he began to chew
the fresh green leaves.
As he did so, he pulled on the vine
and of course, this made the bell ring.
Ding dong! Ding dong! it rang,
high up in the tower.

The King heard the bell ringing.

"Someone in the town needs my help," he said.
So he sent one of his men to find out
who was ringing the bell.

The man hurried into Atri.
When he got to the tower, he saw Stefano
chewing the green leaves.
He laughed as he watched the old horse.

"It's only a horse," he said
and laughed again.
But then he saw how thin and sad
the old horse looked.

He ran back to the palace and told the King.

"A poor old horse is ringing the bell," he said.

The King went to the tower and watched Stefano eating the vine leaves.

"This is the thinnest, weakest horse I have ever seen," he said. "How did he become so hungry?"

"The horse is called Stefano," said one of his men. "His master Antonio has sent him away because he is too old to work any more."

The King was very, very angry.

"Go and bring this cruel man to my palace,"
he told the man. "And take the horse
to my garden. Give him something to eat."

Antonio was very happy because
the King had sent for him.
Perhaps the King would give him
a bag of gold, he thought.
But when he saw the King's face,
he was afraid.

"Look in my garden," said the King.
"Tell me what you can see."

Antonio looked out of the palace window.

"Stefano!" he cried. "My horse Stefano!
Why is he here?"

"He is here because you sent him away,"
said the King. "Why did you do
such a wicked thing?"

"I sent him away because he was too old
to work," said Antonio. "I sent him
to find food for himself."

21

"How could a poor old horse find grass in the streets of Atri?" said the King.
"Will your children send you away when you are too old to work?"

"No," said Antonio.

"Then you must not do such a thing to a poor old animal," said the King.
"You are a cruel, wicked man."

Antonio was very sorry for his cruelty. He took Stefano home and gave him a warm stable and plenty of food. And Stefano lived happily with Antonio for the rest of his life.

Cinderella

Once upon a time there was
a very beautiful girl called Cinderella.
She lived with her father and
her two ugly step-sisters.
Her step-sisters were very unkind to Cinderella.
They wore beautiful dresses, but
she had to wear ugly, torn clothes.
Her step-sisters made fun of Cinderella
because of her old clothes.
They called her Cinders and
made her do all the work.

One day Cinderella was sitting by the fire.
She was tired and hungry and she was crying.
Suddenly she looked up and she saw
a beautiful lady holding a magic wand.

"I am your fairy Godmother," said the lady.
"Why are you crying, Cinderella?"

"My sisters have beautiful dresses,"
said Cinderella. "They have gone to a party at
the palace, and they will meet the Prince.
I will never be able to do that."

"Go and find a big pumpkin,"
said her Godmother. "Then bring me six mice."
   Cinderella did as she was told.
Then her Godmother waved her magic wand and
suddenly the pumpkin turned into a golden coach
and the mice turned into six white horses.
   "Now you can go to the party,"
said her Godmother.

"But I have no clothes to wear,"
said Cinderella.

So her Godmother waved her magic wand
again and suddenly Cinderella was wearing
a beautiful dress of silver.

"Now you can go to the party,"
said her Godmother. "But remember,
you must leave before the clock strikes twelve."

"I promise, I promise," said Cinderella.

So off she went to the party in the
golden coach, pulled by the six white horses.

"How beautiful she is,"
said all the people at the party.
    Then the Prince saw her and
fell in love with her straight away.
They danced together the whole evening.
    Suddenly Cinderella heard
the clock begin to strike twelve.
She remembered her promise and
ran out of the palace.
She got in her golden coach and went home.
    When her ugly sisters came home,
they told her all about the party and
the beautiful girl in the silver dress.
They did not know that it was Cinderella.

The next day there was another party
at the palace.
Off went the ugly sisters and
left Cinderella in the kitchen.
Then her Godmother appeared again.
    "You look sad," she said.
    She tapped Cinderella's dress with her wand
and it turned into a lovely golden gown.
Then she changed her dirty shoes
into glass slippers.
The mice became horses again, the pumpkin
turned into a golden coach and
this time a rat became a coachman.

"Don't forget to come home when
the clock strikes twelve," said her Godmother.

"I promise," said Cinderella and
off she went to the party.

She danced all evening with the Prince,
who was more in love with her than ever.
Suddenly she heard the clock strike twelve.
She had forgotten her promise!

She ran out of the palace and down the steps
and one of her glass slippers fell off.
Cinderella did not stop.

Her coach had turned into a pumpkin again and
the horses and coachman had turned back into
mice and a rat.

Cinderella ran home without stopping.

Her ugly sisters came back and
told her what had happened.

"The beautiful girl left one of her
glass slippers behind," they said.
"The Prince said he is going to find the girl
who can wear it and then he will marry her.
He is going to send his servants
all over the country and every girl must try on
the glass slipper."

The prince's servants went everywhere looking
for the girl who could wear the glass slipper.
Then one day they came to Cinderella's house.
The two ugly sisters laughed with joy.
First one tried on the slipper, but
it was far too small.
Then the other tried on the slipper, but
it did not fit her either.

"Let me try," said Cinderella, but
the ugly sisters laughed at her.

"You!" they said. "You! You are too poor and
dirty. It won't fit you!"

But the prince's servant said, "Every girl
must try on the slipper."
So he gently put the slipper on
Cinderella's little foot. It was a perfect fit!
The ugly sisters were very cross, but
Cinderella did not mind.
    She went to the palace, where
the Prince was waiting for her.
They were married the next day and
lived happily ever after.